MW01639961

Under the Kissletoe

Under the Kissletoe

CHRISTMASTIME POEMS

J. Patrick Lewis

ILLUSTRATIONS BY
Rob Shepperson

Honesdale, Pennsylvania

For Ajax, Hopper, Sanay, and Selis,
my four best presents.
Love, Grandpat—*J.P.L.*

For Anna and Nina—*R.S.*

Printed in China
Designed by Helen Robinson
First edition

"Mrs. S. Claus" first appeared in *Christmas Poems*,
edited by Myra Cohn Livingston, Holiday House, 1984.

LIBRARY OF CONGRESS CATALOGING-IN-PUBLICATION DATA
Lewis, J. Patrick.
Under the kissletoe: Christmastime poems / J. Patrick Lewis ; illustrations by
Rob Shepperson.
p. cm.
ISBN-13: 978-1-59078-438-9 (alk. paper)
[1. Christmas—Juvenile poetry.] I. Shepperson, Rob.
II. Title.
PS3562.E9465U53 2007
811'.54–dc22
2006038984

Wordsong
An Imprint of Boyds Mills Press, Inc.
815 Church Street
Honesdale, Pennsylvania 18431

Contents

If I Had Nothing Else to Do, I'd Write a Christmas Card to You

If I had nothing else to do … ,

I'd write a Christmas card to you
But send it off to someone who,
Say, lived in Millinocket, Maine,
And very carefully explain
That he should quickly mail it on
By way of Portland, Oregon,
And when it got there they would know
To forward it to Buffalo,
New York, so that some person there
Would have to send it first-class air
To Boston, Mass., and back again
By overnight delivery …
then
From Nashville, Tennessee, to Knox-
ville, c/o Auntie's P.O. box,
So she could zip it Fed Express
To your Chicago, Ill., address.
And someday, maybe mid-July—
A Christmas card! You'd wonder why
It took so long to get to you!
I'd call you up and tell you, too … ,

If I had nothing else to do.

A Brown King

Once a brown king
From a brown land
On a brown camel
Out of brown sand

By a great star
And a great heart
With a great love
Played a great part

Rode a small gift
To a small King
In a small stable—
No small thing.

Now the King slept
While the king knelt
And the King dreamed
What the king felt

That a new life
From a new birth
Shines a new light
On a new Earth

Snowflake Star

Call me on the ☎
And tell me that you took
A February ❄
And pressed it in a 🕮.

Then wait till next December.
Now open it again
To the 🗋 your ❄
Was printed on, and then

What you'll 👓 is something
Nobody will believe—
A ❄★! The perfect
🎁 for Christmas Eve.

Donder and Blitzen

This pair of deer
  Nuzzles tonight
Not out of fear.
  Tomorrow's flight

Thrills them! Just now
  They shudder so,
Forgetting how
  Far they must go,

How far they've gone
  Across the years—
A Marathon
  Of Hope—frontiers

As far away
  As frozen Nome,
Alaska. May
  They rest at home,

Hay stablemates,
  These famously
Celestial greats,
  Content to be,

As muzzles touch—
  Antlers entwined—
Two pretty much
  One of a kind.

One Winter Night

When Moon
is pinned
to Sky,
and Wind
begins
to stroke
thin chim-
ney smoke,
and ice
trees click
clickety
quick … ,
there comes
a man
by caravan
of star-
light deer,
who's landing …
here!

The Gingerbread House Song

Chocolate nougat gates and shutters;
Pretzel sticks to build the fence;
Licorice twister spouts and gutters.
Deck the doors with peppermints!

Chewing gum in place of shingles;
Shredded wheat for hay and grass;
Candy pebbles on Kris Kringle's
Chimney; cellophane for glass;

Silver balls for indoor lighting;
Gumdrops make good evergreens;
Walnut roof and almond siding;
Here and there, blue jelly beans;

Graham cracker floors beneath you;
Ice-cream cone—a Christmas spruce.
If inclined to make a wreath, you
Decorate some pfeffernuesse.

Marshmallows to build a snowman.
Looking for a change of pace?
Chicklets, M&M's, and oh, man,
Red Hots brighten up the place.

Mrs. S. Claus

A woman named Mrs. S. Claus
Deserves to be heard from because
    She sits in her den
    Icing gingerbread men
While her husband gets all the applause.

Why Santa Sometimes Prefers the Front Door

He remembers
    Those Decembers
Burning embers,
    Chimney holes,

    When he splendid-
    ly descended,
    But rear-ended ...
    On the coals!

Winter Scene

Th
i
s
cottage
weaves a scarf of
smoke. The horse speaks
only winter steam. Around
the border rounds the silvered
vista of a frozen stream. Two
children angel-wing the snow,
where trees bow down, icicle-
bent. And all across this
picture show, I am your
Christmas or-
na-
m
e
n
t

Under the Kissletoe

A miss'll know
To kiss hello—

The kiss'll go
With mistletoe.

The miss'll glow
For this'll show

That bliss'll grow
From kissletoe.

What Everybody Wants for Christmas

The Mouse wants a slice of Limburger cheese.
The Bird wants a box of Jujubes.
The Squirrel wants a honey-roasted nut.
The Fish want chocolate sprinkles, but
The Cat wants a dish of the old eggnog.

"Give me the mailman," growls the dog.

Ten-Point Snowman Inspection

✓ Will he say he was born a Snowflake's son?
✓ Does he feel that life's too short?
✓ Would he love spring's look of a robin-hood?
✓ Would he laugh at the weather report?
✓ Will he wave at dawn to the paper boy?
✓ Does he miss not having knees?
✓ Does he mind wearing a shoulder crow
✓ Or a black cap of chickadees?
✓ Can he say he's always neatly packed?
✓ Can he stare at the sun unmoved?
If so, Inspector Snow will stamp him

SLICE OF ICE,
INSPECTED TWICE:
MERCHANDISE
APPROVED!

Santa's Summer Vacation

Eight reindeer fly
    Across July
To get suntanned
    In surf and sand.
They spread the news
    In Santa Cruise
Where movie queens
    In limousines
Cure Mrs. Claus's
    Winter blahs,
While Santa laughs,
    Signs autographs—
Love, Santa C.
    His fantasy?
To dip a toe
    In that big o-
cean, knowing they
    Can holiday,
And just this once,
    For two whole months,
Enjoy themselves
    Without the elves.

If I Could Visit England

I would be one happy kid,
I would be a girl who did
Everything her parents said,
Even, "Amber, time for bed!"
    If I could visit England.

    If I could visit England, I
Would see Big Ben up in the sky,
And ride a double-decker bus
(Me, Mom, and Dad—the three of us).

    If I could visit England, we
Would say, "Good day, Your Majesty,
Enjoyed the Guards at Buckingham!"
And words like *bobby, bloke,* and *tram.*

    But most of all I want to go
On Christmas Day with lots of snow,
When opening presents would occur
At least six hours earlier!
    If I could visit England.

Why Do Parents Want to Ruin Everything?

At midnight on the dot,
I hear my father humming.
How could he have forgot
That Santa Claus is coming?

I listen till my head
Hurts, hoping he will hurry
And get back into bed
When there's another worry—

My mother's laughing now,
"Read the directions, honey."
He says, "I don't know how."
But why is that so funny?

And what can children do
When they get sleepy waiting
For noisy parents who
Are not cooperating?

Try this: Believe again
In promises he's keeping.
He'll land here only when
This little boy is *s l e e-*

Purrlibelle

In all her golden days I never saw
a nine-lives wonder like our Purrlibelle,
now ironing my lap with her gray fur.
Her feline age is pretty hard to tell.

Weighing a cloud, she sofas down to dream,
reliving old cat fights through twitch and stir.
Our Christmas Day's unwrappings are all done,
except my homemade Fat-Cat Calendar.

In every Snapshot-of-the-Month she sleeps
on top of me. December's different. Look.
She's licking Santa's sugar-cookie dish
(when Santa wasn't watching, my mom took

that picture). Now she's yawning. Purrlibelle,
who always thinks she is the biggest cheese,
uncurls and murmurs what we tell ourselves
are cat-thanks for the Christmas memories.